WALTO

STAYING
AT HOME

by Heather Maisner and Parwinder Singh

W

It was the last day of school and

Maya couldn't wait for the holidays to begin.

Every year, Mum and Dad rented

a lovely cottage by the sea, and soon

they would be going there again.

A photo of the cottage leant against

the mirror in Maya's bedroom. Every time

she brushed her hair, she stared at the small

white cottage. It had a large back garden

with lots of apple trees.

"Only two more days until we go!" said Maya

that evening, as they sat down to dinner.

Mum said, "I can't wait to get there.

We can walk by the sea every day."

"And we can go for bike rides," said Dad.

"We'll build a tree house, right Maya?"

said her brother Taj.

"I'll pick apples and make apple pies,"

said Granny.

But the next day, as Maya was getting ready

in her room, she noticed a big red spot

on her forehead. There was another

on her nose and a third on her chin.

As she stared, she saw more and more spots

on her face and neck. Her body began to itch.

Maya pushed up her sleeve.

Her arm was covered in spots.

The doctor came. She looked at Maya and said, "You have chickenpox. You must stay indoors for at least a week so that other people don't catch it."

"I can't!" said Maya. "I want to go to the cottage."

Maya's eyes were sore, her head ached, and her body itched all over. She had spots behind her ears and in her mouth.

She felt terrible.

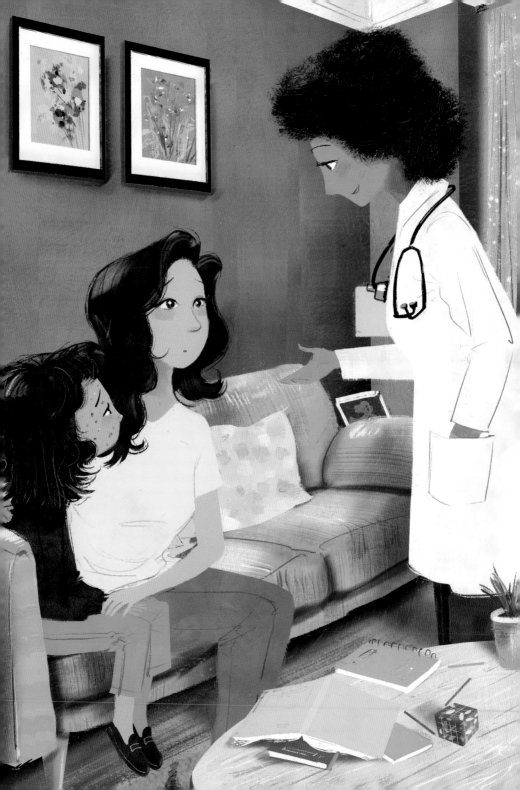

The next time Maya looked in the mirror,

she began to cry.

"The spots are everywhere!" she said.

"I can't go away."

"Never mind," said Granny. "I'll stay here

with you. I'd love to look after you."

"But I really want to go to the cottage,"
said Maya.

"Well, you can go next year," Granny said.

"This year, let's stay home together and
have a special time, just us."

The following day, Maya waved goodbye to her family. Then she ran to her bedroom and cried and cried.

When Maya smelled food cooking, she began to feel hungry and slowly walked downstairs. Granny had made fresh vegetable soup for lunch.

Then she read Maya a story and told her about when she was a child. "I had six brothers and sisters. We never went on holiday," Granny said. "I didn't go to the seaside until I was grown up. But we had good times when we were children. We made things and we played together."

Day by day, Maya started to feel better, but the spots didn't stop itching.

"Don't scratch," Granny said, "or the marks will stay with you forever. We need to keep those fingers busy. Let's do some cooking."

"Can we make flapjacks?" asked Maya.

Granny smiled and nodded.

Maya weighed out the ingredients.

Granny heated the butter in a pan, and

Maya stirred everything together.

The next day, Maya felt even better and some of her spots had started to clear up. She and Granny made bread. Maya weighed the flour and butter, added the yeast and salt, and mixed it all together with warm water. She loved kneading the dough and seeing it rise in the warm cupboard. She made a perfect loaf.

Each day, Granny showed Maya
how to make something new.
The week went by very quickly.

When her family returned, Maya ran to greet them.

"The car broke down and it took hours to get there," said Dad.

"It rained all week," said Mum. "We only went to the beach once."

"I had no one to play with," Taj moaned. "And it was too wet to build a tree house."

"Well, I've been busy," Maya said.

She pointed to the bread, flapjacks, brownies

and fairy cakes she'd made.

"I didn't know you could cook!" said Dad.

"Nor did I," Mum said.

"I had a great time," Maya said.

"Do you know, when Granny was little,

they baked every day and they always made

their own cakes and puddings and ..."

"Will **you** bake every day?" asked Taj,

eating his second flapjack.

Story order

Look at these 5 pictures and captions.
Put the pictures in the right order
to retell the story.

1

Maya learns how to bake with Granny.

2

Maya says goodbye to her family.

3

Maya has chicken pox.

4

The family come home.

5

The family are excited about their trip.

Independent Reading

This series is designed to provide an opportunity for your child to read on their own. These notes are written for you to help your child choose a book and to read it independently.

In school, your child's teacher will often be using reading books which have been banded to support the process of learning to read. Use the book band colour your child is reading in school to help you make a good choice. *Staying at Home* is a good choice for children reading at White Band in their classroom to read independently.

The aim of independent reading is to read this book with ease, so that your child enjoys the story and relates it to their own experiences.

About the book

Maya is very excited about her family's annual trip to the cottage. When she is suddenly struck down with chicken pox, she must make the most out of missing the trip.

Before reading

Help your child to learn how to make good choices by asking: "Why did you choose this book? Why do you think you will enjoy it?" Ask your child about what they know about chicken pox. Then look at the cover with your child and ask: "How do you think the girl feels in this picture? Where do you think she would like to be rather than at home?"

Remind your child that they can break words into groups of syllables or sound out letters to make a word if they get stuck.

Decide together whether your child will read the story independently or read it aloud to you.

During reading

Remind your child about what they know and what they can do independently. When reading aloud, support your child if they hesitate or ask for help by telling them the word. If reading to themselves, remind your child that they can come and ask for your help if stuck.

After reading

Support comprehension by asking your child to tell you about the story. Use the story order puzzle to encourage your child to retell the story in the right sequence, in their own words. The correct sequence can be found on the next page.

Help your child think about the messages in the book that go beyond the story and ask: "Why do you think Granny was a good person to stay home with Maya during her illness?"

Give your child a chance to respond to the story: "Which part did you like the best? Why?"

Extending learning

Help your child predict other possible outcomes of the story by asking: "What if the holiday hadn't gone badly for Maya's family? How might Maya have responded if they came home with a good report?"

In the classroom, your child's teacher may be teaching about different kinds of sentences. There are many examples in this book that you could look at with your child, including statements, commands, exclamations and questions. Find these together and point out how the end punctuation can help us understand the meaning of the sentence.

Franklin Watts
First published in Great Britain in 2020
by The Watts Publishing Group

Series Editors: Jackie Hamley, Melanie Palmer and Grace Glendinning
Series Advisors: Dr Sue Bodman and Glen Franklin
Series Designers: Peter Scoulding and Cathryn Gilbert

A CIP catalogue record for this book is
available from the British Library.

ISBN 978 1 4451 7224 8 (hbk)
ISBN 978 1 4451 7225 5 (pbk)
ISBN 978 1 4451 7230 9 (library ebook)
ISBN 978 1 4451 7930 8 (ebook)

Printed in China

Franklin Watts
An imprint of
Hachette Children's Group
Part of The Watts Publishing Group
Carmelite House
50 Victoria Embankment
London EC4Y 0DZ

An Hachette UK Company
www.hachette.co.uk

www.reading-champion.co.uk

Answer to Story order: 5, 3, 2, 1, 4